# TREASURE ISLAND

**By Robert Louis Stevenson**

**Retold by
ANGELA WILKES**

**Illustrated by
PETER DENNIS**

Series editor: Heather Amery

He stopped at the inn. "Many people here?" he asked. Jim shook his head. "Then this is the place for me," said the captain.

Long ago a boy called Jim Hawkins lived alone with his mother on a wild stretch of English coast. She kept the "Admiral Benbow" inn.

One windy day a sea captain came up the road, singing a shanty, "Fifteen men on the dead man's chest! Yo ho ho and a bottle of rum!"

He gave Jim a silver coin. "I'll give you a coin every month if you keep a sharp look-out for a sailor with only one leg," he said.

The captain's name was Billy Bones. He soon became well known at the inn for the dreadful stories he told about wicked pirates.

He stayed at the inn for month after month but never paid Jim's mother any money. She was too scared of him to ask for it.

One winter's morning, when Billy Bones was out, a stranger came to the inn. "Is there a captain staying here?" he asked.

Suddenly he saw Billy Bones coming along the road. He pushed Jim into the inn and dragged him behind a door. "Keep quiet," he hissed.

Jim was very scared. Billy Bones came in and walked across the room. "Good day to you, Captain," growled the stranger.

Billy Bones spun round. His face went pale and he looked as if he had seen a ghost. "You remember me, don't you?" asked the stranger.

3

"You are Black Dog," gasped Billy Bones. "Yes," said the stranger. "We have business to discuss." They sent Jim for some rum.

Suddenly Jim heard shouts and the sound of chairs being knocked over. He ran back into the room. The men were drawing their swords.

Billy Bones lunged at Black Dog, then chased him out of the inn. Black Dog fled, blood pouring from a wound in his shoulder.

Suddenly Billy Bones gasped and clutched his chest. He was having a heart attack. He fell to the ground and Jim ran to help him.

Bones had to stay in bed after his attack. He called Jim. "You must help me," he whispered. "Cap'n Flint's pirates are after me."

"They want something I've hidden in my seaman's chest. If ever you see any strangers around, you must call the law at once."

Time went by and Jim saw no suspicious strangers. Then one cold, foggy day he saw a hunched old man coming slowly up the road.

The man was blind and tapped the road with a stick. When he reached the inn he stopped and called out, "Where am I?"

"At the 'Admiral Benbow' inn," said Jim. The blind man grabbed his hand. "Take me to Billy Bones," he hissed fiercely.

Frightened, Jim led him inside. "Here's a friend come to see you, Captain Bones," he said. Billy Bones looked up in terror.

"Hold out your hand," said the blind man. He hobbled up to the captain, pressed a note into his hand and hurried out of the inn.

Bones read the note. "The pirates are coming at ten," he said. He jumped up but suddenly gasped and fell down. He was dead.

5

Jim and his mother were scared about the pirates coming to the inn. But Jim's mother wanted to find Billy Bones' money.

They ran to the village to ask for help. But everyone was too scared of pirates to go back to the "Admiral Benbow" with them.

So Jim and his mother crept home on their own. When they reached the inn they rushed inside and locked all the doors and windows.

Then they looked for Billy Bones' money. Jim found a key round Bones' neck. "This could be the key to the chest in his room," he said.

He and his mother ran upstairs to Bones' room. The key fitted the chest, so they quickly unlocked it and threw open the lid.

The chest was full of odd things – clothes, trinkets and pistols. Underneath Jim found a packet of papers and a heavy bag.

The bag was full of money. "I'll take what I'm owed," said Jim's mother, and they began to count the coins. Suddenly they stopped. Some one was rattling the door of the inn. Then they heard the blind man's stick tap down the road. "Quick," said Jim. "We must go."

They took the money and papers and fled from the inn. Then Jim heard people coming. He pulled his mother into a hiding place.

A band of men broke down the inn door. As they ran through the house Jim heard shouts of "Bones is dead" and "Find his chest!"

Suddenly the blind man threw open the window of Billy Bones' room. "The papers have gone!" he shrieked. "Find the boy!"

The pirates searched the whole inn for Jim, then met outside. Suddenly they heard a whistle. "The warning!" one of them cried and they raced towards the cliffs. A group of soldiers galloped over the hill. They had heard that Jim and his mother were in danger.

The pirates ran to a cove where a boat was waiting. The soldiers chased after them but they were too late. The pirates had escaped.

"The pirates were looking for this packet of papers," Jim told the captain of the soldiers. "We should take it to Squire Trelawny."

The captain took Jim to the Hall, where Squire Trelawny was dining with Dr. Livesey. They were very surprised to hear Jim's story.

Dr. Livesey opened the packet. In it was a map of an island. Next to a cross on it was written: "Most of treasure here."

# The Map of the Island

The map showed that the island was nine miles long and five miles wide.

It had two sheltered inlets and a hill in the middle, called "The Spy Glass".

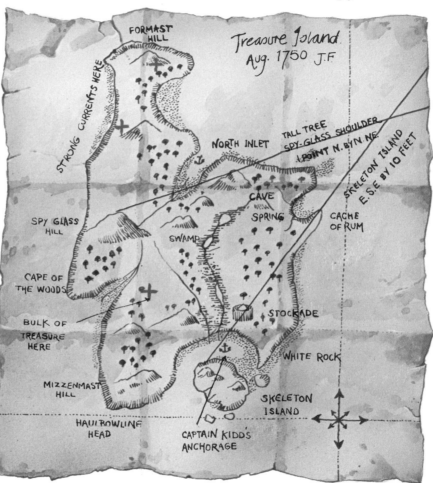

"This shows where Captain Flint's treasure is buried," he said. "No wonder Flint's crew were after Billy Bones. They wanted this map!"

The squire was excited. "I'll find a ship and crew and we will sail to the island," he said. "But we mustn't tell anyone about the treasure."

On the back of the map was more writing:

The silver is in the northern hiding place. Follow the east hill ten fathoms south of the black rock with a face on it.

The weapons are buried beneath the sand dune on the north point of the north inlet cape bearing E and a quarter N.

A month later Jim said goodbye to his mother and left the inn. He went to Bristol and met Squire Trelawny at the harbour.

"There's our ship," said the squire, pointing. "She's called the *Hispaniola*. I've picked a good crew for her and we sail tomorrow."

Jim had to take a message to the landlord of a nearby inn. He was called Long John Silver and he was to be the new ship's cook.

Long John was friendly, but Jim saw that he only had one leg. "Bones told me about him," he thought, "but he's too nice to be a pirate."

Jim went back to the squire and found Dr. Livesey with him. They rowed out to the *Hispaniola*. They were very excited about the voyage.

On board they met Captain Smollett, the ship's captain. "I thought everything about this voyage was to be kept a secret," he said angrily.

"Now I find that all the crew know exactly where we are going and that you are after Flint's treasure. I don't trust any of them."

The squire and Dr. Livesey were worried to hear this, but it was too late to find a new crew. The next day the *Hispaniola* set sail.

Jim soon became friends with Long John. Long John had a parrot he called Cap'n Flint, after the famous pirate who had died.

One night Jim went on deck and climbed into a barrel to fetch an apple. Suddenly he heard men near him talking very quietly.

It was Long John whispering to a sailor. "I was Cap'n Flint's right-hand man," he said. "All his crew were afraid of me."

"Join us pirates," he went on. "We may live roughly and risk hanging, but we make lots of money. One day we will all be rich."

"This voyage seems much more exciting now," said the sailor, "I'll join you." Long John laughed wickedly and they shook hands on it.

Jim was horrified. Captain Smollett had been right not to trust the crew. They were plotting mutiny. How many of them were pirates?

A third man came along. It was Long John's friend, Israel Hands. "How long are we going to wait before we strike?" he grumbled.

"We'll wait until we have the treasure," said Long John, "then we'll kill the captain and all the loyal members of his crew."

Just then the moon rose and there was a cry of "Land ahoy!" Everyone rushed on to the deck. An island loomed in the distance.

"Have any of you been here before?" asked the captain. "I want to know a safe place to anchor." "I've been here, sir," said Long John.

The captain showed him a chart. Long John looked at it eagerly, but the treasure was not marked on it. He pointed to an inlet.

While the crew were busy, Jim went up to the doctor. "I must talk to you in private," he whispered. "I have some terrible news."

The doctor hurried away. A few minutes later Jim was called to the captain's cabin. He told his friends what he had heard.

"It's too late to turn back now," said the captain. "We must find out how many men are on our side and be ready for trouble."

The next morning the *Hispaniola* anchored in a wooded inlet. It was very hot and the island looked gloomy and forbidding.

The men had to work hard all day and were grumbling. Long John looked worried. Captain Smollett was afraid that the crew would rebel.

He called them together. "It's been a hot day and you are tired," he said. "You can take the afternoon off and go ashore."

The men cheered and ran to the boats. Jim decided he wanted to go ashore too. When no one was looking, he slipped into one of the boats.

Jim's boat was the first to reach the island and Jim jumped ashore. Long John called out after him but Jim pretended not to hear and ran into the trees.

"Join us pirates," he hissed. The sailor shook his head. Suddenly they heard a scream. It sounded as if someone was being killed.

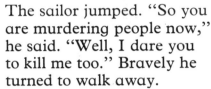

The sailor jumped. "So you are murdering people now," he said. "Well, I dare you to kill me too." Bravely he turned to walk away.

He was exploring the island when he heard footsteps. He hid behind a bush and peered out into a clearing. Long John was talking to one of the sailors.

Long John whipped the crutch from under his arm and hurled it at the sailor. It hit him so hard, he fell down dead instantly.

Jim was terrified. He did not wait to see what happened next but ran as fast as he could from the scene of the murder.

Jim ran for a long time, then a sudden noise made him stop. He looked round and saw a shadowy figure dodge behind a tree.

Jim's heart jumped. What was following him? Was it a man or a bear? He felt in his pocket for a gun and crept towards the tree.

Suddenly a wild man stepped out and knelt down. "Don't shoot, I'm poor Ben Gunn," he said. "I haven't spoken to a soul for three years."

"My pirate friends left me here to die," he went on, "but I'm still alive and now I'm rich. What are you doing here?" he asked Jim.

Jim told him what had happened. "Tell the squire I can help him and make him rich if he helps me to escape from here," said Ben.

Just then they heard the sound of a cannon. "I must go back," said Jim. He and Ben ran to where the ship was anchored.

16

Meanwhile, back on the ship, the doctor found Jim was missing and was worried. He rowed ashore with one of the men to look for him.

Not far inland they came to a stockade, a log house surrounded by a strong fence. The house was on a hill and could be easily defended.

Suddenly they too heard the scream. "The trouble has begun," said the doctor. "We must fetch the others and barricade ourselves in here."

They returned to the ship and loaded a boat with guns. They set off for the shore but the boat was overloaded and began to sink.

There were some pirates left on the ship and they loaded the cannon. The squire shot at them and they fired the cannon.

The squire's men reached the shore safely and ran for the stockade. Long John's men on the island heard the firing and chased after them.

As Jim ran to the ship he heard the gunfire and saw the Jolly Roger, the pirate's flag, flying from the mast. Then he saw the captain's flag hoisted over the stockade and knew his friends were there. He crept through the woods and scrambled over the fence.

The doctor and the squire were pleased to see him. Jim told them about Long John killing the sailor and about meeting Ben Gunn.

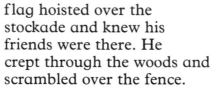

Jim's friends looked grim. They did not have many guns. They decided to stay in the stockade for the night and fight the pirates.

Next day there was a cry of "Flag of Truce." To everyone's surprise, Long John was hobbling up the hill, waving a white flag.

"I'll make a deal," he told the captain. "Give us the chart and stop shooting and we'll let you on the ship and take you to a port."

18

"I'll not bargain," said the captain. "Surrender and I'll take you home to a fair trial. Otherwise we fight on." Silver limped angrily away.

When he had gone, the captain gave orders to prepare to fight. The men took up positions and waited. It was a very hot day.

Suddenly shots rang out and a band of pirates ran out of the woods towards the stockade. As they swarmed over the fence, the squire's men opened fire.

In the fierce battle that followed, both pirates and loyal sailors were killed. Suddenly the fighting was over and the last pirates fled into the woods.

The squire walked round inside the stockade. Five pirates and two of his men had been killed, and Captain Smollett was badly wounded.

Dr. Livesey bound the captain's wounds. Then he took the chart and went into the woods. "He's gone to find Ben," thought Jim.

Jim could not bear the sight of the dead and wounded. When no one was looking, he took two pistols and slipped away into the woods.

He wanted to look for a boat Ben Gunn had built. He walked quietly down to the shore and saw Long John rowing away from the ship.

He crept along the beach until he found a big white rock Ben had told him about. Hidden beneath it was a small goatskin tent.

Jim lifted a corner of the tent and found Ben Gunn's boat there. It was a coracle, a round boat made of thick sticks and goatskins.

Now Jim had a new idea. He decided to paddle out to the ship and cut it adrift. He lifted the coracle and took it down to the water.

He launched it into the waves and got in, but found it hard to steer. When he tried to paddle, the boat just spun round and round.

But luckily the tide swept the coracle towards the *Hispaniola*. Soon Jim saw it looming up out of the darkness in front of him.

Jim came alongside the ship and caught hold of the anchor rope. Slowly he cut through it. Suddenly he heard shouting on board.

He lifted himself up to a porthole and looked inside. Israel Hands and another of the pirates were struggling in a terrible fight.

The ship began to turn and Jim dropped back into the coracle. He was very tired and fell asleep as the coracle drifted out to sea.

When Jim woke up he felt hot and dazed. It was already day and the coracle was tossing on the waves off the coast of the island.

There was a line of jagged rocks between Jim and the beach, so he paddled on, hoping to land his boat further along the coast.

Suddenly, right in front of him, Jim saw the *Hispaniola* skimming across the waves. All at once she turned and her sails went slack.

No one seemed to be steering her. Jim wondered where the sailors were and paddled towards the ship, hoping to board her and take her over.

Again the ship turned and headed straight for him. Just as the ship crushed the tiny boat, Jim sprang up and caught hold of the boom.

One sailor was dead. The other one groaned and Jim ran to his side. It was Israel Hands. "What are you doing here?" he muttered.

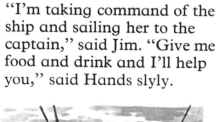

"I'm taking command of the ship and sailing her to the captain," said Jim. "Give me food and drink and I'll help you," said Hands slyly.

He swung himself on to the ship and looked round. To his horror, he saw two sailors lying in pools of blood on the deck.

Jim took down the Jolly Roger and threw it overboard. Then he bandaged Hands' wounds and they sailed for the northern inlet.

When they got there they had to wait a while for the tide to turn. "Will you go below and fetch me some wine?" asked Hands craftily.

Jim did not trust Hands. He went below, ran to the far end of the ship and looked out. He saw Hands crawl across the deck to some rope

and take out a long, rusty dagger. Hands felt its blade, then hid it under his jacket and crawled back to his place. Jim had seen enough.

He took Hands some wine and Hands swigged it down, pretending to be very weak. "We'll sail the ship in now," he whispered hoarsely to Jim.

As Jim was sailing the ship into the inlet, a sudden noise made him turn. Hands was behind him, knife in hand, ready to strike him.

He lunged at Jim, but Jim nimbly leapt to one side and Hands hit his chest on the tiller, which winded him for a few seconds.

Jim quickly took out his pistols. He aimed and tried to fire them, but there was only a dull click. He had forgotten to load them.

Hands threw himself at Jim again and Jim dodged behind a mast. Hands chased Jim round the ship, but Jim was too quick for him.

Suddenly the ship tilted and Jim and Hands were thrown on to the deck. Jim leapt to his feet. He had to find a new way of escape.

He sprang up the mast ropes, but Hands slowly hauled himself up after him. Terrified, Jim loaded the pistols. "Come no further or I'll shoot," he cried.

Suddenly Hands threw the dagger and it pinned Jim's shoulder to the mast. As Jim cried out with pain, the pistols went off. Hands screamed and fell into the sea.

Jim clung to the mast. His shoulder was very painful. Bravely he pulled the dagger out and climbed shakily back down to the deck.

He slipped overboard into the shallow water and waded ashore. "Now the ship is ready for the captain again," he thought happily.

He set off across the island towards the stockade to look for his friends. As he came near the house he could see the glow of a big fire.

He crept into the house. No one was on watch and Jim could not see in the dark. "Pieces of eight," a shrill voice suddenly called out.

It was Long John's parrot. "Who's there?" called Long John. Jim turned to run but someone grabbed him and held up a light.

"Look who's here," said Long John. "You'll have to join us now. Your friends have given you up and gone away. Or would you rather die?"

"I don't have much choice," said Jim bravely, "but if you spare me I will help you when you return to England and are tried for piracy."

Snarling, one of the pirates drew his knife and sprang at Jim, but Long John stopped him. "I give the orders round here," he said.

The pirate stepped back and the others gathered round him. "Let's go outside," said one and they went out, muttering angrily.

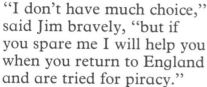

"I'm in trouble," Long John whispered to Jim. "The ship has gone. But at least the doctor gave me the chart." Jim was astonished.

The pirates came back. One of them stepped forward. "We want a new leader," he said. Long John said nothing, but held up the chart.

The pirates whooped joyfully. They had not known about the chart. They passed it round, shouting, "We'll be rich after all!"

Next day Dr. Livesey walked into the stockade. He had come to tend to the wounded pirates. He was very surprised to see Jim.

Jim apologised to him for deserting his friends and told him where the ship was. "Don't worry," said the doctor. "We'll save you."

He went over to Long John. "There'll be trouble when you look for the treasure," he said. "Take care of Jim and shout if you need help."

When the doctor had gone the pirates set off to look for the treasure. They were all heavily armed and carried picks and shovels.

The chart said the treasure was buried beneath a tall tree on Mizzenmast Hill. As the pirates climbed the hill they argued about which tree it could be.

The pirates stared at it in silence. Then they heard a strange, high voice: "Fifteen men on the dead man's chest," it sang.

The pirates were terrified. "It's Flint's ghost," they gasped "It's only someone trying to scare us,'" Long John said calmly.

Suddenly one of the pirates yelled. The others ran over to him. There, at the foot of a tree, lay a human skeleton which was pointing towards the top of the hill.

The pirates struggled on up the hill. At last they saw a tall tree in front of them. They charged towards it, then stopped in their tracks.

A huge hole had been dug at the foot of the tree. Some one had got there before the pirates and all of the treasure had gone.

Long John secretly gave Jim a pistol. "Stand by for trouble," he whispered. "He is always changing sides," thought Jim.

The pirates jumped into the hole and began digging. One of them held up a coin. "Did we come all this way just for this?" he roared.

He climbed out of the hole. "Down with Long John," he cried. Suddenly shots rang out from the bushes and two of the pirates dropped dead.

The next minute Dr. Livesey and Ben Gunn rushed into the clearing, their guns smoking. The three pirates still alive ran away.

"Quick," cried the doctor. "We must head them off before they reach the boats." They charged down the hill with Long John hobbling along behind them. They reached the beach before the pirates, knocked a hole in one boat and pushed out to sea in the other.

As they rowed to the ship, Dr. Livesey told Jim that when Ben Gunn was alone on the island he had found the treasure. He had dug it up and taken it to his cave.

"When I saw the ship had gone," said Dr. Livesey, "I led our friends to Ben's cave. I heard Silver's plans to find the treasure and came to rescue you."

They left one man on board the ship to guard it, then headed for Ben's cave. It was enormous. Great heaps of coins and gold bars glinted in the firelight.

The squire and captain were very pleased to see Jim safe. That night they and the loyal sailors had a huge feast to celebrate finding Captain Flint's treasure.

First published in 1982 by Usborne Publishing Ltd, 20 Garrick Street, London WC2 9BJ, England.

Printed in Belgium

Next day they loaded the treasure on to the ship. Then they sailed away with Ben and Long John, leaving the three pirates on the island. Soon they reached South America and hired a new crew. Here Long John escaped with a sack of gold. He knew he would be hanged for piracy if he went back to England. The squire and the doctor sailed home and gave Jim some of the gold. He never forgot his adventure on Treasure Island.